Dear Andrea,

To one who shares the same aesthetic as me — a great love for a very cute cat! She is Artistic Kitty!

Very best wishes, blessings and much love to you and Ho — I couldn't be happier for you both. He is wonderfully lucky to have found you, and of course he is one of my oldest, dearest friends, so you too are blessed.

Love,
Adrianne

Hello Kitty® Through the Seasons!

PHOTOGRAPHS AND HAIKU

Concept and Photographs by
Jennifer Butefish and Maria Fernanda Soares
Text by Kate T. Williamson

ABRAMS IMAGE

INTRODUCTION

Hello Kitty loves nothing more than enjoying a beautiful day. Whether she's stopping to smell the flowers or pausing to paint them, she always celebrates the wonder of nature!

Each season brings new and exciting adventures to share with her family and friends. She loves picnicking in the spring and sunbathing in the summer; hiking in the fall and snowboarding in the winter. Hello Kitty reflects on all of her feelings and memories by writing a special haiku every day.

Join Hello Kitty as she captures the magic and beauty of the seasons. No matter what the weather may be, Hello Kitty's heart is filled with love all year long.

Spring

A butterfly lands—
our sandwiches half-eaten,
she stays for dessert.

Baking with the sun,
I add sugar, eggs, and milk—
and a pinch of love!

At one with my board,
on an ocean of concrete—
time for an ollie!

In the dappled grove,
a capricious tree sparrow,
I fly back and forth.

Punch-filled champagne flutes–
beneath the pink canopy,
I'm lost in your eyes.

Earth caught in my cleats—
though my true goal is friendship,
I won't let you score!

Sorry, tomatoes!
Onion, carrot, you are next!
Stir-fries are hard work.

Dreaming of the stage,
I work on my extension—
a pink rose in bloom.

White dove poised for flight—
does this hat obscure my bow?
I pose patiently.

A gust of spring wind
sends my friend far above me.
I know she'll return.

Summer

Fresh from the garden,
ambassadors of summer
meet in my tummy.

A warm summer breeze—
on this perfect afternoon,
I catch a pink cloud.

Staring politely,
I float above a starfish
and avoid the sharks.

Although it is night,
my sidewalk garden sparkles
with bright fire-flowers.

Despite the aces
and my many strong returns,
I'll always have love!

The white foam lingers
on its way back to the sea,
letting me go first.

Tired of watching,
the sun glints through the palm fronds
and dances with me.

Basking in the sun,
I sweetly wave to sailors—
look out for the rocks!

In the hot, still air
I emerge without thinking—
a serene kitty.

The waves creep closer
to refresh me with a splash—
they can't surprise me!

Pampered by the heat,
on the cedar boards I rest,
dreaming of salad.

The mountains and I
enjoy our time together—
I'm filled with great peace.

One crisp, green apple
for breakfast or my teacher?
Next time I'll bring two!

K-I-T-T-Y!
I think the game is over—
someone help me up!

Cicadas buzzing—
I listen to the river
and release my catch.

Such a busy day!
When I'm done mending fences,
I'll go for a ride.

While the fire crackles,
I concentrate on toasting.
More chocolate, please!

In my chilly loft,
the flowers reassure me:
spring will come again.

Five cleanly split boards!
If it weren't for my prowess,
this belt would be pink.

Autumn afternoon—
a leaf hurries to the ground
to join an acorn.

Ensconced in pink plush
on a cozy Friday night,
I wait for my friends.

Testing one, two, three!
Please have my cupcakes ready—
ginger ale, no ice.

Winter

Storm of white sugar—
a wintery confection,
I sit happily.

The barren branches
now adorned with tasty treats—
Sugar Plum Kitty.

Two eyes just like mine
and a scarf and bow to match—
I've made a new friend.

Whiskers flecked with frost—
despite this frozen climate,
my life is quite sweet.

The snow keeps falling.
Though I'm dressed for winter fun,
I hope it will melt!

It's too cold to shop!
No need to think of sizes:
my friendship fits all.

Gift wrapping is fun,
but gift giving is better—
where are my reindeer?

A swan in winter,
gliding on the frozen lake—
how I'd like to fly!

My favorite day!
Filled with love and chocolate,
I wait for next year.

Watching from above,
I will keep you from all harm—
Guardian Kitty.

Editor: Tamar Brazis
Design and illustrations by Celina Carvalho
Production Manager: Kaija Markoe

Concept and photographs by Jennifer Butefish and Maria Fernanda Soares
Text by Kate T. Williamson
The majority of Hello Kitty®'s clothes, shoes, and accessories were provided by Build-a-Bear Workshop® and are available at www.buildabear.com.
With special thanks to the following Sanrio designers:
Janessa Lazon, Sachiho Lee, Carlos Mansilla, Alma Mejorado, Cheri Messerli, and Peggy Perez

Library of Congress Cataloging-in-Publication Data

Williamson, Kate T. (Kate Tower), 1979—Hello Kitty through the seasons / text by Kate T. Williamson ;
concept and photographs by Jennifer Butefish and Maria Fernanda Soares.
p. cm.
ISBN 0-8109-5993-3
1. Hello Kitty (Fictitious character)—Juvenile poetry. 2. Children's poetry, American. 3. Seasons—Juvenile poetry.
4. Haiku, American. I. Butefish, Jennifer. II. Soares, Maria Fernanda. III.Title.

PS3623.I569H45 2006
811'.6—dc22
2005026809
ISBN 0-8109-5993-3

IM▲GE
Published in 2006 by Abrams Image,
an imprint of Harry N. Abrams, Inc.
115 West 18th Street
New York, NY 10011
www.abramsbooks.com

Printed and bound in China
10 9 8 7 6 5 4 3 2 1
Abrams is a subsidiary of

LA MARTINIÈRE
GROUPE